In the end, there's a plane crash

J. Sharpe

www.jsharpefiction.com

D0639668

Copyright © 2020 by J. Sharpe

In the end, there's a plane crash

Translator: Lisa Rijnhoud

Cover design: hummingbirdbookcovers.com

First, a small gift

I want to thank you personally for buying this book. You love to read, otherwise, you wouldn't have bought this book. So let me give you an exclusive free story.

In this story the main character reincarnates in to a flower and finds herself in some strange situations.

To get access simply go to my website www.jsharpefiction.com.

How it began

Kevin

Warningly, the steward put his hand on Kevin's arm. Kevin had already had three whiskeys before boarding and two beers and a glass of wine during the flight. He didn't get more from those bastards. Didn't the guy know how much he was struggling? Kevin saw everything through a haze, and he wanted to keep it that way. At that moment, there was nothing worse than being sober. Alcohol kept reality at bay, like an invisible shield.

His plan was simple. He had come up with it the day after his last hospital visit. He would leave everything and everyone behind and travel to a warm place where nobody knew about his existence. There, he would find a nice place to put an end to his life. Far away from his wife, son, friends and colleagues, before his illness would kill him. Kevin had always seen himself as a brave and proud man. If there was one thing he hated, it was the way others looked at him: pitiful. He knew all of them – well, most of them anyway – meant well. But he could not take it. It would be better for everybody if he would just die, but he wanted to do so in his own terms.

But from the moment the plane left the ground and started to pierce the clouds, he began to doubt his decision. He had just disappeared. He had not left a note or anything like that. His family was probably going crazy with anxiety right now. *You are being so selfish.*

Indeed.

But wasn't this the best thing he could do for them? Was it not better for his wife and son to simply go on with their lives? To just, one day, find out that he had died, that the suffering was over, instead of sitting at his bedside for weeks or months until the disease would finally take him? He was doing this for them.

You keep telling yourself that.

This was the reason why there was just one thought running true his mind at the moment: *Need. More. Alcohol.*

If he wanted to continue with this, he had to completely get rid of his thoughts about his family.

"I just want another beer." He spoke the words with a double tongue. He staggered and had to hold himself up on the headrest of chair 3C. "And if you don't want to get it for me, I'll get it myself."

"For the last time, sir," the flight attendant said while the aircraft trembled because of turbulence. His voice was just a bit louder than the sound of the engines. "If you don't sit down now, I will be forced to take measures and ..."

"Just give me a freaking beer!" Kevin's stomach protested. He collapsed, hit his forehead hard on the top of the backrest of one of the chairs and fell on the floor.

It immediately went black before his eyes.

Linda

Although the passengers, of course, didn't know any better, Linda was not allowed to call herself a stewardess just yet. She was in her last year of her flight attendant training and was here as part of an internship. Normally, companies did not allow unqualified personnel on their planes, but because the company she now flew with closely worked together with her school, she was allowed to be here.

It was Linda's first flight. If it was up to her, it would also be her last.

Never in her whole life had the realization that she had made the wrong choice struck her so fast. It felt like a slap in the face. As a little girl, she had dreamed of seeing the world. When she had gone on holiday with her parents and the plane flew above the clouds, she couldn't imagine that there was a better job than being a flight attendant. She only had one problem.

She hated people.

It was a problem that really came to light two years ago, around her seventeenth birthday. Of course, even before that, she had always been an outsider. It was something she partly attributed to the fact that she was half Chinese and therefore looked different from everyone else. She didn't have many friends and she could be annoyed by others when she walked down the street and saw what certain people were wearing or saying. More and more she started to notice that she had to bite her lip so she wouldn't approach those people and ask what the hell was wrong with them. Her parents didn't know about all this. They were far too busy with their own failed lives - they both had been divorced three times and one of them even lived in Italy at the moment. They, therefore, did not notice that their daughter had a sophisticated lack of empathy. At least, that's what her doctor called it. It was the doctor who had advised Linda to enroll in a different study. But she persisted. She would be a flight attendant, no matter what. She just needed to find a way to deal with people, that's all.

But now, after more than three hours in the air, she saw how stubborn she had been and the mistake she made. Within just a couple of hours, the reality had ruined her dream. She could live with the lack of space on the aircraft, or the fact that she was surrounded with nasty smells all the time, constantly heard the hum of the engines, felt the pressure in her ears, and the fake smiles that her colleagues gave her and the passengers. But what she couldn't take was the constant whining of those same passengers.

Could I have some peanuts and something to drink?

How high are we actually flying?

At what time will we arrive?

Do you perhaps have a pillow for me?

That, and the two crying babies on board.

The screams had already started before the plane took off in Amsterdam and it had continued almost without interruption. Linda wasn't good at ignoring sounds. She had started to get a headache. In her mind she had seen herself approach the babies a dozen of times to grab them and slap them on the floor until they were dead. In real life she just smiled at them and their mothers and fathers when she passed them in the aisle.

Linda had walked to the front of the plane, when a man, seated on the aisle in chair 52C, held out his hand to get her attention. The expression on his face told her that he had not had the most pleasant flight so far.

"Do you know by chance how long it will take to get to the gate when the plane has landed?" the man asked. "I have an important appointment that cannot be missed. And since we left Amsterdam half an hour later than intended ... "

The man and the woman who sat next to him looked at Linda questioningly but didn't say anything.

Linda suppressed a sigh and continued to smile. The corners of her mouth started to hurt. "I'm sorry, sir, but I don't have that information. It depends on which runway we end up on. Madrid only has four, so it probably won't take too long."

The man snorted. "As soon as we land, you have ten minutes to get me to the gate, do you hear me? Otherwise, I will file a complaint. I'm a lawyer and ..."

Amber, dressed in the same blue uniform as Linda, stood less than sixteen feet further up the aisle and had picked up the conversation. She approached them. "We will do our best, sir," she said to the man. Then she put an arm around Linda's shoulders. With light force, she led her back toward the workspace in the back of the plane. When they arrived, Linda squirmed out of her colleague's grasp.

"What did you do that for? I was perfectly able to handle the situation myself. I'm a big girl. I don't need protection."

Amber crossed her arms. "I didn't protect you for him but rather the other way around." She pointed to Linda's hand.

Linda looked down. She had her hand clenched. "I wouldn't have hit him or anything."

"Really? You sure about that?"

Hell no. But she would never admit that. "What makes you say that?"

"I've been watching you for the last few hours, Linda. That's my job as your internship supervisor. And to be honest, I don't like what I see."

"What are you talking about? I did everything you asked of me."

A woman came out of the toilet just a couple of feet from them. She looked at them. Amber smiled at her and the woman walked back to her seat. When Amber continued the conversation, her voice almost was a whisper. "It's not so much about what you do, but more about what you don't do. It's the look on your face. We are locked up in a metal tube with almost one hundred and fifty people. You can't act like you love it up here. People pierce right through it. I have already received several complaints about you." She sighed. "And it is precisely this type of attitude that makes me wonder if you are suitable to be a flight attendant."

There it was. Until now, Linda had held herself up, but now that her bubble had been punctured with a blunt point, she could no longer hold up the facade, not even for herself. "Fine. I don't want to be one anyway." She screamed so loudly that the people in the back rows shockingly looked in their direction. "I want to go home as soon as possible. I'm done. Done with this plane, done with all the shitty passengers and done with you!" She walked away and before Amber could stop her, she had locked herself in the toilet.

The knock on the door came almost immediately.

"Linda?"

Linda, sitting on the toilet, couldn't hold back her tears.

Amber kept knocking on the door. "Come on, Linda. Don't do this. Open up."

Linda would rather die than obey.

Arnold

"What was that all about?" Arnold just came back from a short walk through the plane. He had needed to stretch his legs for a moment. He looked towards the end of the aisle at the toilet cubicle and the stewardess that was banging her fist on the closed door.

"Looks like that young thing has locked herself up." Frank already turned back around. With his elbow resting on the armrest and his chin resting on the palm of his hand, he looked out of the window. "I wouldn't be surprised to hear if she has a burnout. Everybody seems to have a burnout these days."

Arnold moved past the empty seat on the aisle side and took the seat next to his husband. "How can a young thing like that have a burnout?"

Frank just shrugged.

Arnold put his hand on Frank's arm. He too stared through the window, hoping to see anything other than the clear blue sky, bright sun rays and clouds beneath them, as far as the eye could see.

Frank grimaced when he shifted his weight to his other but cheek. "Next time we'll definitely take the car if we want to go to Spain."

Arnold laughed. "It will take us at least four times longer to get there."

"Is that so? Don't forget that although the flight may only take a few hours, you have to add the time it takes to travel from our home to the airport, where we lost three hours checking in and boarding. Instead of that hassle, we could have enjoyed the surroundings of beautiful landscapes. And my legs would have had more room. I feel like a fucking sardine, stuck in a can."

Arnold grabbed Frank by the chin, turned it in his direction, and kissed his lips. "I love you."

Now it was Frank's turn to grin. "Why yes, try to kiss it away, don't you?"

"We've already had this conversation. You have never flown before and wanted to give it a try."

"Well, I have tried it out now, haven't I? Again, next time we will take the car."

And with that, the conversation was over.

Frank put his head against the wall next to the window and closed his eyes. It didn't take him long to fall to sleep and after everything they had experienced in the past two months, Arnold didn't find this strange. Frank was exhausted, just like he was. If there was one couple anxious to go on a vacation ...

On the other side of the aisle, a blond girl with two ponytails said: "Iew. Mom, those two men kissed each other."

Arnold turned his head towards the girl and looked at the mother with interest, curious as to how she would react. "Acceptance starts with education," his father had always said. Arnold had always taken that saying to heart.

The mother — in her forties, skinny, in a colorful dress — saw his gaze, smiled almost apologetically, and turned to her daughter. "And what do you think about that, Kimberly?"

Her daughter – Arnold estimated her to be about six years old – was noticeably overwhelmed by the question and looked straight ahead as if the answer would appear on the screen in front of her.

"Do you find that strange?" The mother persevered.

The girl shrugged her shoulders.

"Do you think it's a bad thing if mommy gives daddy a kiss?"

"Not a bad thing, it's just gross." On the side of the window sat a boy. Probably the brother. His thick spectacles told Arnold that he was pretty short-sighted. He had short, red hair and, like his sister, freckles. Arnold estimated him to be around fourteen years old. He was holding a paperback and kept his eyes on the pages while talking.

"You are married," the girl answered, neglecting her brother. "Then it's okay."

Arnold, impressed by the mother's handling, smiled, raised his hand and showed his wedding ring.

The mother immediately responded. "Look. They are married too. But even if they weren't, would you have a problem with them kissing?"

Kimberly had to think about that. After a few seconds, she said, "No." She put earplugs back in her ears and tapped the screen in front of her with her fingers to resume the paused movie. End of conversation.

A static hiss came from the speakers above their heads, and, as far as Arnold could see, all the displays in the back of the seats froze.

The pilot's voice was calm and businesslike. "Good afternoon, ladies and gentlemen. Here's your captain speaking. As you may have noticed, we have started the decline. Because we had to adjust our route slightly so that we didn't end up in bad weather, we will arrive about fifteen minutes later than planned."

Somewhere further in the plane, a man began to swear loudly. "You bastard. I have an appointment!"

The pilot continued undisturbed. "We hope that it won't interfere with your plans. If someone needs any assistance, please contact our ground staff. Our expected arrival time is five past eight in the evening, local time. It's currently cloudy in Madrid, but it's expected that they will disappear in a few hours. On behalf of KLM and all of my colleagues, I wish you a pleasant stay and we hope to see you again soon."

There was a sharp click and the movies on the screens started playing again.

A *ping* sound filled the atmosphere and the 'fasten seatbelt' sign lit up above their heads. Almost immediately, Arnold heard clicking sounds around him as most passengers did what the sign asked of them.

Arnold looked out of the window and saw that the plane was about to cut through the clouds. He also fastened his seatbelt again, checked Frank's – who apparently hadn't loosened it to begin with – and looked toward the aisle again. His gaze lingered on the boy, who hurriedly turned another page of his book. His mouth was slightly open and his eyes were large, as if in disbelief. Visibly confused, he glanced up and back through the gap between two seats. He then carefully studied the pages of the book again.

"May I ask what you are reading?"

The boy looked at him. His eyes were fearful.

His mother answered for him. "I think it's a short story collection. Right, David?"

David didn't respond. He just looked at the book in disbelief.

From where he was sitting, Arnold was barely able to see the books cover. On it was a picture of a burning plane, surrounded by creatures that looked like ghosts. "Horror stories about airplanes?" Arnold looked at the mother with incomprehension.

She only casually shrugged her shoulders. "David loves horror stories."

Kimberly agreed. Apparently, her earplugs were nothing more than a disguise and she had heard the entire conversation. "He has already finished all the Stephen King's books."

"You don't say," Arnold responded.

"It's true," Kimberly answered.

Great parenting, mom. Just look at that kid, he's scared to death.

But it was not his place to say anything, so Arnold merely said: "Well, you are a brave one kid, if you are able to read that right now. I wouldn't want to read a horror story about an airplane when I'm on one."

"You see, Daphne." The voice came from behind Arnold. It sounded heavy and reproachful.

So, the father is here too.

"I'm not the only one who thinks he shouldn't be reading that right now."

The mother waved his comment away. "Oh, just leave him be."

David flipped a few pages back, reread something, and then looked at his mother with his eyes wide open. His face was almost as white as the pages of the book in his hands. His voice was a barely intelligible whisper. "I think the plane is going down."

Due to the constant buzzing and the noise around them, Arnold was not entirely sure whether he had understood the boy correctly.

"What did you say?"

An elderly man with a curly mustache and dressed in a suede jacket just came out of the toilet in the middle of the plane and was kindly requested by one of the stewardesses to go back to his seat and fasten his belt. The man nodded and started to walk back to his seat again, but he was only able to walk slowly and take small steps. The stewardess followed him, gently forcing him to pick up the pace. She continued to smile, though you clearly could see in her eyes that she was annoyed.

Further down the aisle, a woman who quickly got up to take something out of her bag in the overhead compartment was pointed to the 'fasten seatbelt sign'.

"I think the plane is going down," David repeated, this time with more urgency in his voice.

"What do you mean, 'going down'?" Arnold asked.

"Calm down," the boy's mother said, trying to calm him. "There is nothing to …"

At that moment the plane suddenly started to move from left to right violently. It made a few huge jumps and immediately fell down a few feet.

The old man in the suede jacket, the woman who wanted to grab something out of her suitcase, the cabin crew and almost everybody else who hadn't yet fastened their seatbelts were thrown roughly through the plane. They hit seats, the overhead storage compartments and some even the ceiling.

People started to scream.

Again, a static noise was heard through the speakers and the movies on the screens froze. But before the captain was able to say anything, a deafening *bang* sound was heard. The front of the plane tilted down so fast that Arnold banged his face against the seat in front of him. A few seconds later the front of the plane came into contact with something else. The screams of his fellow passengers were drowned out by a scraping noise that sounded like metal on metal. The plane started shaking wildly.

Arnold wanted to scream, but simply couldn't. His heart was racing so fast that he could feel it beating in his throat. His hands were sweaty, and he saw black spots in his vision. His face hurt from the blow against the seat in front of him earlier, especially his mouth and right cheek. He tasted the metallic flavor of blood. He glanced out through the window.

Did the plane land?

He simply didn't believe what he saw. From where he was sitting, he had been able to see a part of the right-wing. Until now. The entire wing was gone, and the plane was still sliding as if the clouds on which they had landed – *wait, what?* – now consisted of ice!

The squeaking and howling sound that came from the belly of the plane was loud and terrifying.

Suddenly, with a last, frantic shock, the plane came to a halt.

After the "landing"

Linda

Linda woke up with her butt on the floor, her head rested against the door of the toilet and her left hand in the bowl. She looked around dazed. She felt ill and the pain in her head was overwhelming. Her body felt like it had been hit by a car. The last thing she could remember was that she had been thrown through the toilet, like a bouncing ball. Moaning, she took her hand out of the toilet, wiped it dry on her uniform, and sat down on her knees. Everything hurt but apparently nothing was broken.

What the hell just happened?

She stretched her arm, unlocked the door, and crawled unto the aisle.

The first thing she noticed was the lack of engine noise. What she did hear was screeching and howling. All the lights were off, so the inside of the plane was covered in shadows.

It was a mess. It was as if a bomb had gone off inside the plane. Several luggage compartments had opened. There were bags and suitcases everywhere. Some had sprung open. The contents were scattered everywhere.

There were some people in the aisle, unconscious or perhaps even worse, but most passengers, those who had listened to the advice and had not unduly loosened their seat belt during the flight, were in their seats and looked around in shock. That was, the passengers who were still there. When they had taken off, they had had one hundred and twenty people on board and almost every seat had been occupied.

Now at least a third of the seats were empty.

In addition to the screeching, Linda heard cries for family members or other travel companions.

An older woman said: "Bill?"

A young woman cried: "Pam? Where are you?"

A boy yelled: "Mama? Daddy? Kimberly?" He held a paperback in his hands.

A man said: "Frank? FRANK?"

And there where many more passengers looking around frantically, in panic.

Linda saw Amber lying in the aisle, only a few meters away. Her head and shoulders lay on the floor, her butt and legs limp over an empty seat. Her eyes were open and glassy. Her skin was pale. But it was mainly her twisted neck that turned Linda's stomach.

Jesus.

Linda screamed.

What ...? How ...?

She gasped and felt lightheaded.

A voice from the speakers silenced everyone. "Hello everybody, my name is Anderson. I'm the co-pilot on this flight. I wasn't sure to what extent I would tell you anything, but I decided to be completely honest with you. It looks like we ..." The voice faltered as if gasping for breath. "... touched something. Captain Hopman is ..." Again there was that unpleasant silence. "... gone."

"Christ, he too?" A man cried.

"Keep it together," a woman said. "I'm sure there is a good explanation for all this. People don't just disappear."

"Then where the hell are they?"

The co-pilot continued undisturbed. "I'm trying to get in touch with, well, whoever, but it looks like all systems are out. The right-wing has broken off completely and all engines are out of order. Not a single meter is working, so I have no idea how high or where exactly we are at the moment, but when I look outside through the windows ..."

Another silence. "It looks like we ... Jesus, I just don't believe I'm going to say this. It looks like we crash-landed on the clouds."

Immediately the hysteria was back. People started screaming and crying.

Although Linda saw all of this from the corner of her eye, she couldn't manage to tear her gaze away from Amber.

She had never seen a corpse.

Kevin

The fact that he had vomited had sobered him up. Well, partly, that is. But at least he was able to stand up. He was still nauseous, but not nearly as badly as when he had poured his stomach contents on the floor.

Now he was standing before the entrance to the cockpit. With him were four men and three women. He stared past a few people, but instead of letting his gaze hang on the hundreds of buttons, outstanding screens, or the shaking co-pilot, he looked out of the windows. He saw a clear blue sky above a field of snow. Because that was what it was.

Now that he had seen it, there was no doubt about it, and he did not understand that he was apparently the only one who understood what it was.

The purser went inside the cockpit and spoke to the co-pilot. "We just lost all the power. Nothing works anymore. And when I say nothing, I mean nothing. It's like all the batteries of every mobile phone, iPad or laptop stopped working."

Kevin grabbed his cellphone from his pocket with a raised eyebrow. The screen remained black, no matter how many buttons he pressed.

Fuck!

Shaking his head, he put the phone back in his pocket.

"We counted how many people are here," the purser went on. "Believe it or not, we currently only have forty passengers on board. There also colleagues among the missing. Linda, that trainee, is the only remaining cabin employee."

There was fearful murmuring behind them.

Anderson looked at the man in shock. "You're kidding me."

The purser shook his head. He looked like all his blood had disappeared from his face. His skin was ash gray. "They are nowhere in sight. And believe me, we searched everywhere. Five of the remaining men, six women and three children – including a baby – didn't survive the crash. Amber is one of them. Twelve passengers are lightly injured, three of whom more serious."

Anderson shook his head in disbelief.

"Did you see how Martin disappeared?" the purser asked Anderson.

"No. And I don't get it. One moment he was still next to me, the next he was gone."

"The captain?" Kevin asked.

Anderson nodded and made another attempt to get his equipment back online. He turned dozens of buttons and pressed another five without any results.

"He can't just have disappeared?" An older woman in her sixties pushed some people aside until she stood in the doorway. She looked around the cockpit suspiciously, as if she did not trust the co-pilot.

Anderson answered with a trace of annoyance in his voice. "If you see the captain, please tell me."

"What do you think happened exactly?" The purser asked.

The vibration in their voices made it clear that both he and the co-pilot did their best to remain calm and professional, but that their feelings were fighting to get the upper hand.

Anderson clenched his fist. "As far as I know, the backside of the plane came in contact with something hard, as a result of which the plane pivoted forward, also hit something and started to slide."

"And what precisely did we hit?" Another man asked.

"It seems to me that the only thing you could hit when you're in the air is another

47

plane," the older woman said. "But if that were the case, none of us would have survived."

"It wasn't another plane," Anderson said.

Curious about how this problem would be solved, Kevin listened to the conversation. At that moment he was more angry than scared. Furious even. "I do hope you don't really believe that we are stuck on a cloud, do you?"

"I believe what I see," Anderson replied.

Unbelievable.

"Do you hear what you're saying?"

The copilot looked at him. "I know what it sounds like, but do you have a better explanation?"

"Calm down," the purser said. "An argument won't solve anything." He stood between Anderson and Kevin and spread his arms. "Nor is it a good idea for you all to come into the cockpit. Mr. Anderson is trained to act correctly in situations like this. Let him do his job."

Anderson looked grim. "Oh yeah. I remember clearly what to do. I think it was the third week of my education as a pilot when we learned what we should do if we get stuck on a cloud."

"Come one, guys!" Kevin said in dismay with an unsteady voice. "What are we talking about? It's snow, nothing more. Nothing less. We probably just crashed somewhere in the Alps."

"We passed the Alps about an hour ago," Anderson replied annoyedly.

"Another goddamn mountain, then."

"It's not snow," said the purser.

"What makes you so sure?"

"Because that's fucking impossible."

"And why is that?" Kevin asked.

"Because right before the crash we were about sixteen thousand feet up. Even if you're right and we somehow ended up on a landscape full of snow, then the crash would have torn this plane apart. And the fall would have lasted much longer then it did."

"He is right," Anderson agreed. "The chances of survival would be close to zero. And look ..." He pointed outside. "It ... is steamy. Snow does not do that."

"You guys have lost your minds, you know that?" Kevin wanted to say something else to them, but then a thought popped up in his head. A thought that was much more important than this crap.

There was alcohol in the backside of the plane. And probably nobody to stop him if he went over to grab some.

That idea pleased him.

Arnold

He tried to swallow the lump in his throat. Tears filled his eyes. They blurred his vision. He didn't mind. On the contrary. It was better to not see or accept what had just happened. Because he simply couldn't accept it. You simply don't crash on a cloud and people don't just disappear. Ten minutes earlier he would have believed that. Now he wasn't so sure anymore.

Arnold looked out of the window, where mist obscured the lower half of the window. The white landscape was endless.

Frank was gone, just like the little girl and her mother on the other side of the aisle. He and the boy – David – were the only two people in this row.

Come on. Keep it together. Breath.

He tried. He breathed in and out, long and deep. It helped. A bit. At least he got some control over his body back.

A man walked down the aisle and passed him. He staggered, crashed into the seat next to David and, muttering to himself, moved on to the back of the plane. The smell of alcohol followed him like it was his shadow.

Arnold put his hand on the headrest in front of him and pulled himself up. His knees were trembling. He looked around the dark cabin and saw men, women, and children among the dozens of empty seats. All of them looked anxious. Frightened. Confused. Like they expected someone to take the lead and tell them that everything would be okay. Arnold saw it in their eyes. He didn't blame them. His eyes probably reflected that same look. He had hoped to hear the reassuring voice of the co-pilot. But it remained quiet. Arnold thought about going to the cockpit to get some answers for himself, but when he saw the group that was already there, he realized that that made little sense. Nobody knew what to do. Anderson was no exception. Also, if there was news, the co-pilot would no doubt share it with them. Even if he would have to do so by standing in the cabin and raising his voice, now that the power was out.

David cried. The paperback was shaking in his hands. It broke Arnold's heart and made him realize that he had to be strong. For himself, for the boy and for everyone else who needed it right now. He went over to the boy and sat down next to him.

"Hey," he whispered. "It will all be okay." His words came out insincerely. Arnold hated himself for it.

David just looked at his closed paperback and sobbed.

Arnold glanced at the book. "David? Earlier, right before everything went haywire, you said the plane was about to go down. Was that a joke?"

The boy shook his head.

"How did you know?"

The boy raised his head and looked at him. His eyes glittered with tears. "I've read it." He opened the paperback and was about to show him something when a shout caught their attention.

"No! Wait, you idiot!"

Arnold scrambled out of the seat with a wildly beating heart, stepped down the aisle and looked at the back of the plane. There he saw the man who had walked past him a couple of minutes before. He stood before the doors. His left hand was clutching an open beer can, his right was on the handle. Right behind him stood a group of passengers who with their voices and outstretched hands tried to convince the man to stay away from the door.

"Think, man," said a bearded man. "Haven't you ever seen an airplane movie? When you open that door a vacuum will arise and suck us all out of the plane."

"At this altitude, the outside temperature must be somewhere around three degrees Fahrenheit," a woman with short curly hair agreed with a panicky voice. "We will freeze as well as fall."

"That won't happen," said a third voice. The young stewardess — Bella's, no, Linda's, Arnold had seen her name on her nametag earlier —gaze rested on a corpse in the aisle. "At this height, the difference in pressure between the outside and inside will make it impossible for him to open that door." She turned to the half-drunk man daringly. "Go on, try it."

The man gave her a stoic look. He emptied the beer can, threw it away, shrugged and pushed the lever down.

The door went open with a creaking sound.

Arnold's mouth fell open. He stood motionless.

A gust of wind blew in the plane, down the aisle, and hit him. It was cool, not cold. A temperature of forty degrees rather than three.

"That's impossible," the stewardess stammered.

A number of men and women came from the other side of the plane, including the purser and the co-pilot. Arnold recognized his uniform.

"What the hell is going on here?" As soon as Anderson saw the opened door, he stopped abruptly. "You can't be serious."

The man who previously had had the beer can in his hands looked around defiantly. "Do you guys believe it now? It's snow. Nothing more than that. We made it to the ground. I'm not sure how, but it's true." He looked at the stewardess. "If we were still in the air, I could not have opened the door, right?" Then, without a doubt, he jumped out of the plane.

People started to scream.

"Has that guy completely lost his mind?" The purser said.

Arnold gasped.

Almost everybody went to the open door.

"Did he fall through the cloud?" Someone asked.

Arnold was pulled by his shirt. He turned his head and saw David looking at him with fearful eyes.

"He's still alive."

"Who?"

"That drunk man. The cloud caught him, just like it caught this plane."

"How do you know that?"

"I've read it."

"Read it?"

David nodded. "In one of the stories. I didn't want to believe it at first, I still don't want to, but everything that happened is described in the third story of the short story collection." The boy opened the book on the right page and handed it to Arnold. "Here, see for yourself."

Arnold looked at the boy with a raised eyebrow.

"Read," David insisted.

Arnold glanced over the pages. Almost immediately his heart skipped. He read the words while he held down his breath, no longer scanning, but absorbing them carefully.

"See?" David asked. "Everything that happened is described there. The stewardess who is locked up in the toilet, the two men kissing each other, the crash, the drunk man opening the door ... everything."

"That's impossible."

"Even the fact that you are reading this now is described." David turned a page. "See?"

Arnold read the sentences with trembling hands.

The boy put his finger halfway down the page and the man absorbed the words in horror. The pain in his chest almost became too much for him. His hand cramped. His throat was suddenly dry. He tried to calm himself down but failed.

"I don't understand. How …?"

It's just like that movie. Just like Inception.

Arnold jumped up. "Anderson!" The co-pilot turned towards him, just like the purser and a few fellow passengers.

"Look at this." Arnold approached them and held the book in front of Anderson.

The purser looked at him. "Can it wait, mister? As you can see, we are dealing with something bizarre here."

"Do me a favor and read these four pages." As if he had run the marathon, Arnold gasped for air again. "Believe me, this is just as bizarre."

The co-pilot reluctantly accepted the book. He looked at Arnold than started to read.

The purser and four others looked over his shoulders and did their best to read too.

Arnold turned and looked at David, whose head rose above one of the chairs, seven rows back. "Do you know what will happen?"

David shook his head. "I wasn't that far yet."

At that moment a crackling and hissing sound came from the speakers.

Impossible. There is no power.

"Did you guys hear that?" A presumably seven-year-old girl with long blond hair stuttered.

Arnold listened carefully.

"What do you mean?" An older man, a few rows back, asked.

David looked at Arnold. "I hear it too."

"Hear what?" the older man asked again.

The girl answered. "Singing children."

David nodded in agreement.

A crackling sound. It was loud and sounded if there were a number of people in the belly of the plane beating against the ceiling.

And again, sounds echoed through the speakers. This time, everyone heard it. It was the sound of a dozen of children laughing. It started as a whisper, but with every second the sound became louder and louder.

Some passengers started screaming.

The sound was so loud that it hurt Arnold's ears. He lost his balance, slammed hard against one of the chairs and crashed to the   floor. Then, suddenly, the laughter stopped and the feeling was restored to his body.

Silence.

Arnold sat down on one of the chairs, put his hand on his painfully thumping head, and looked puzzled at the speakers in the ceiling.

"Oh, Jesus," he heard a woman say. She was sitting a few rows in front of him. "It's Marleen. She's in the hold. She is talking to me."

Someone else said: "It's my husband. He is begging me to help him."

Everybody started to panic.

Arnold too heard a voice.

Frank: *"She's here with me, my love. In the hold. She's so sweet, so beautiful. Exactly as she looked before she died."*

A second voice let Arnold realize who Frank was talking about.

"Daddy?"

Arnold looked around in shock. "Julia?"

Their adopted daughter had died two months ago. Leukemia. They found out too late. She had been only four.

A shiver ran down his back. Arnold shouted.

"We have to get to the hold." He was just about to get up and force Anderson – or anyone else – to listen to him, when something warm dripped on his head.

Arnold brought his fingers to his crown. Again, he felt a drop. It stuck to his fingers. When he held his hand in front of him, he saw that the liquid was a dark red, almost black. Without realizing what he was doing, he brought his finger to his mouth. The metallic taste made his stomach turn.

Now the drops fell on him faster. They had a nauseating odor, like that of decaying meat.

A screeching sound made people scream.

Arnold looked down the aisle and nearly choked. The blood not only dripped from the speaker above *his* head but also from all the others. It even dripped from the edges of the storage compartments. The only thing was that it was no longer dripping. It was gushing out like a waterfall. Within a matter of seconds, there was a layer of the liquid on the floor, at least a couple of inches thick. And it continued to rise! If it went on like this, the plane would be completely filled with the sticky substance within a few minutes.

That is not possible. There is an open door. It should be able to flow. Why isn't that happening?

Arnold realized that he had to do something. If he stayed here, he would drown. Apparently, he was not the only one with that thought. Everybody looked around in panic.

There was only one place they could go.

Kevin

He had estimated that the jump from the plane to the snowy ground was about thirteen feet. He landed on something soft, like a pillow, and immediately felt weightless.

He had to admit he had been wrong. Whatever this stuff was, it wasn't snow. But it wasn't made of clouds either. Snow consisted of ice crystals. This was something different. Something softer and warmer. He was right in the middle of it now. The white stuff came up to his waist.

The plane was badly damaged. He could clearly see it from where he was standing. There were black stripes on the bottom. Where the wing was supposed to be, now only a ragged protrusion of ten feet could be seen. The wing itself was gone without a trace. It was probably hidden somewhere in the clouds.

Kevin took a few steps back until he was able to look through the door. He saw his fellow passengers, and some of them also saw him. He could barely hear their surprised voices.

He looked away. Rays of sunlight warmed his face.

It was so relaxing out here. So peaceful. A breeze blew through his hair. He could imagine a worse place to spend his last days.

This was way better than a warm country. If only Clara and Steven could see this. He should call them. He…

His hand slid to his pocket and pulled out his cell phone when it came to mind that it wasn't working. So, he was surprised to see the photo of him and his family behind the seven apps of this home screen. The three lines at the top right indicated that he still had a signal.

How was this possible? What the hell was going on here?

It doesn't matter. Call them, Kev. It's time to say goodbye the right way. Maybe this is your last chance.

The clouds hit him playfully. He found the desired number and brought the phone to his ear. Somebody picked up after three rings.

"Dad?" The line crackled.

Kevin smiled. There were tears in his eyes. "Hey, little man."

More crackling sounds.

"Are you coming home? Mom is sad. She doesn't know where ... "

"I love you, kid." Kevin interrupted.

A short silence followed.

"I love you too. But ..."

"Is mommy around?"

"Yes."

"Can I talk to her for a moment?"

There was another silence.

Then he heard her voice. "With Clara."

"Hi, honey."

"Kevin?" Her voice was peppered with anger and uncertainty.

"It's me."

"Where are you?"

"You wouldn't believe me if I told you."

"Are you drunk?"

"Just a little."

"I can hear it in your voice."

"I'm sorry, Clara. I couldn't say it in your face."

Clara broke. "Say what? That you are incurably ill?"

Her words were like slaps across his face. His mouth fell open. "You know about that?"

"Of course, I know, Kev," she cried. "I spoke to your doctor, just like I spoke to the police, where I reported you missing. And I get it. I really do. I understand why you thought running away would be the best thing for us. But …" She went silent.

"I…" Kevin stuttered.

This time there was reproach in her voice. "That choice wasn't completely yours to make, Kev. Not you alone determine what's best for your family and who will grieve for you. That's just not how it works."

"Listen, Clara."

"Come home."

"I'm not sure if I can."

"Why not?"

"Wait, I'll show you." He turned toward the plane and held out his cell phone, ready to take a picture. At that moment he saw that a black-red substance was dripping from the open door and that people were letting themselves fall out of the plane. What surprised him the most, however, was that they did not surface again. They fell right through the "clouds". Their screams left little to the imagination.

"Kevin?" Clara's voice could be heard from somewhere in the background.

Kevin was too surprised to say anything in return.

Linda

The blood continued to flow from all holes and cracks. There was a loud buzzing in the hold. Dozens of voices sounded from the speakers, indefinable.

They had to make an impossible decision. Stay in the airplane and drown or jump out onto the clouds. Seven men, three women, and two teenagers had chosen the latter, but as soon as it had become clear that they were going right through the clouds, falling to their death, the stream of people at the door stopped. Everybody stayed as far as they could from the open door.

Linda's heart ached painfully. Panic made her eyesight hazy. She could smell her own sweat. She was covered in blood splatters and stood up to her knees in the cold drab.

The level kept rising.

Like most passengers, she crawled onto one of the seats and made herself as small as possible. "Please, let it stop," she screamed.

Anderson was now the only one in the aisle, clearly petrified. What the hell was he doing with a paperback in his hands? He was trained to act correctly in panic situations like this. He should do something. Why wasn't he doing anything?

Arnold

It suddenly became clear to him. No matter how bizarre and unreal, there might be a way out of this hell.

Arnold jumped into the aisle. Immediately, the blood flowed into his shoes and soaked his socks and pants. It was almost high enough to reach his shirt.

Half-walking, half-swimming, he approached Anderson, who was looking around motionless. His eyes where big. Without saying anything, Arnold grabbed the paperback out of his hands, made his way back to David – who was screaming up on his chair – and pushed the blood-stained paperback into his hands.

"Read the story."

The boy looked appalled at him. "What?"

"This shitshow started with that story."

"You're joking. Do you think this all ends if I finish the story?"

"You can at least try."

"People have disappeared," the boy cried. "The aircraft is full of blood, we are on a cloud and the plane is damaged. What do you expect to happen?"

"Just read the goddamn story."

Arnold climbed onto the chair next to the boy and took his shaking hand. "Come on, David. What do we have to lose?"

The boy had to think about that. "I don't know if I'm capable of reading right now."

"You can do it. And I'll read it with you."

For a moment, the boy kept staring at him, as if Arnold had lost his mind.

Maybe that was the case.

Yet, they opened the book, looked for the right page, and started reading aloud.

Kevin

The plane just disappeared. One moment the aircraft was clearly visible, the next it disappeared spontaneously. At the place where the plane had been standing just a second before, there now was a void.

It took Kevin a few seconds to realize that the metal tube had fallen through the clouds.

Clara was still on the telephone. "Kevin, say something."

He too began to sink away in the cloudy substance, painfully slow. At first, he thought the clouds were slowly rising above him, but he soon came to the conclusion that the ground was no longer solid. It had turned into a sort of quicksand. He thought of the people who had jumped out of the plane and had gone right through the clouds and wondered why he or the plane hadn't fallen through before. What made him so different, so special? Was there actually a reason for it? Were some parts of the cloud solid and did he just happen to be at the right place? Was it dumb luck? Luck that had now abandoned him?

Did it matter?

His legs were now hanging under the cloudy substance. He felt them dangling in the void. An icy cold swept through the fabric of his pants. Under the substance, he would no longer be protected against the cold.

"Take good care of our little man, Clara," he said.

"Kev?" Clara screamed. "Don't you dare hang up on me, do you hear me?"

He continued to sink. His waist disappeared into the clouds, followed by his belly ...

"I've always loved you, honey," he said. "Always remember that."

"Kevin? Kev!"

His arms fell through the clouds. The cold sensation felt like thousands of needles penetrating deep into his skin. He uttered a cry of pain and lost his grip of his cell phone, which made the long journey to earth. Kevin knew he would soon follow. He also knew that the fall would not last long.

That gave him comfort.

In the end, there's a plane crash

Eight kilometers outside

of Bilbao, Spain

The undamaged paperback was some sixteen hundred feet away from the nearest, still burning, piece of the airplane. He slowly absorbed the blood on his cover. It fed him, just as he had been feeding himself with blood and souls for decades. All the passengers on the plane were now a part of him. New pages, new letters, in his ever-growing body.

There were sounds in the distance. Sirens. But something else as well. Footsteps? No, voices.

"Good Lord ..."

"How awful ..."

"All those people ..."

A boy's voice. He came closer. "There is something here."

The book felt how fingers touched his body. Through the tough of the skin on his cover he knew who the kid was. Diego. Fifteen-year-old. Spaniard. His parents owned the land on which the plane had crashed. They had heard the bang and had called the emergency services.

The book felt that it was being opened. Diego was unable to read the Dutch text that the book was currently showing. That was a pity. Now the boy couldn't unravel what had really happened. Now the book couldn't receive honor for his work. On the other hand, maybe it was for the best. After all, the book could now make a new story. This time in Spanish. About a boy in the countryside, his parents and a very special farm.

Sometimes the book had to wait months or even years before it was picked up and opened again. Sometimes the souls just forced themselves on him one after the other, like now. It was something to be thankful for. He had to enjoy it and had decided to do so.

As the boy closed the book again and walked away with him in his hands, the book was already beginning to rearrange his letters. He was already looking forward to the moment that he would be read.

Can you help?

Thank You For Reading My Book!

I really appreciate all of your feedback, and I love hearing what you have to say.

Reviews are very important for an author. When I get more reviews on my books it allows them to stay more visible, so I can spend more time writing rather than marketing. So if you want me to put books out more quickly, please leave a review on this one!

The review doesn't have to be long. Just a few words and some stars is enough to help me out.

Thank you so much!

J. Sharpe

Nobody will survive the new plague!

Angels: they're among us. I would know. There's one trapped inside of me. But the image you probably have of these "helpers of God" is wrong, I guarantee it. They are all maniacal assholes.

Anna Meisner awakes, naked and afraid, tied to a chair in a dark room. Across from her sits a woman who is her spitting image. With tears in her eyes, the woman puts a gun against her head and kills herself. Anna is not found until days later and in a state of hypothermia, moments from dying. But when she wakes in the hospital, she finds that the police don't see her as a victim, but as a suspect. It's the beginning of a series of catastrophic events in which she has no choice but to play a part. Is this the end of humanity?

Eden (nominated for a Bastaard Fantasy Award) is a post-apocalyptic suspense novel. If you like fast-paced books with a lot of twists and like to search for all the hidden references of the bible, then you will definitely love this book.

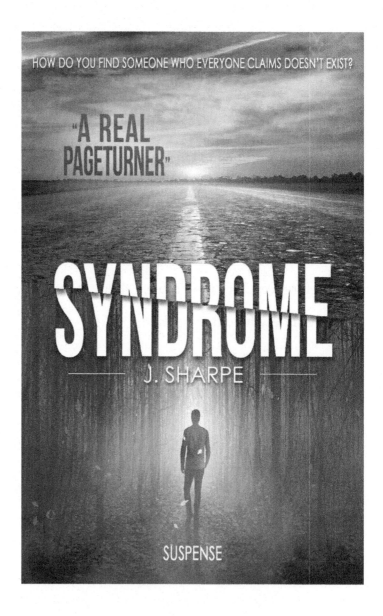

HOW DO YOU FIND SOMEONE WHO EVERYONE CLAIMS DOESN'T EXIST?

"A REAL PAGETURNER"

SYNDROME

J. SHARPE

SUSPENSE

How do you find someone who everyone claims doesn't exist?

It starts as a game but ends in terror. Soon it becomes clear. Someone is chasing them.

After an accident, Peter's mother is in a coma and his father is unable to cope. Because of this, Peter has no other choice than to drop out of school, start a job and take over the care of his little sister. One day he picks her up from school to take her to the mall. Then the unthinkable happens. They're being followed. And their pursuer is not from this world…

When his sister disappears, Peter starts to notice that more things are terribly wrong. Especially when no one seems to remember her. Even his father claims he never had a daughter. It's almost as if she never existed...

Will he be able to save his sister? Or is she lost forever?

Syndrome is a suspense novel that keeps you on the edge of your seat. If you like fast-paced stories, with plot twists that keep you surprised with every turn of the page, then you will definitely love this book by award nominee and bestselling author J.Sharpe.

Syndrome was nominated for a Harland Award and A Bastaard Award.

Pick up Syndrome today, if you dare!

J. SHARPE

TREEHOUSE

A treehouse isn't always a safe place to play!

When Grace is driving on the highway with two screaming eight-year-olds in the back seat, she's frustrated to say the least. So when she sees a sign for a Rest Area, she's more than happy to pull over. The boys see the treehouse first. And when they climb its ladder, it's already too late. Then the screaming begins.

Treehouse is a free short suspense/horror story. An introduction to the works of award nominee and bestselling author J. Sharpe.

Download the book now, if you dare.

From the Amazon Bestselling Author of Eden and Syndrome

J. SHARPE

RETURN

a short story

Michael has a lot of explaining to do.

It's been one hundred and twenty years since his employer left for vacation. Ever since then, he's been in charge. Right before she left, his employer gave him an assignment. He had to find a solution to the fact that heaven was getting full.

But things have gone so wrong. Michael made decisions that affected the world, and potentially his job, in a terrible way.

Return is a magical realism short story with lots of references to religion. If you like funny, short stories than this book by award nominee and bestselling author J.Sharpe is definitely for you.

Pick up *Return* today for free!

About the author

J. Sharpe – a pseudonym for Joris van Leeuwen (1986) – has written several mystery thrillers, fantasy novels, and short stories.

His work is often compared with novels by authors such as Stephen King, Dean Koontz, and Peter Straub.

He was shortlisted for the prestigious Dutch sci-fi and fantasy Harland Award in 2016 and 2018, for the best fantasy book written in that year.

He is known for not sticking to one genre only. His thrillers, for example, usually contain elements of horror, sci-fi, or fantasy, and vice versa.

Made in the USA
Monee, IL
16 July 2020

36622649R00062